S0-AVG-041

A

B

Dedicated to the memory of my adventurous sister, Deb.

10 9 8 7 6 5 4 3 2 1

Published in 2006 by Lark Books, A Division of
Sterling Publishing Co., Inc.
387 Park Avenue South, New York, N.Y. 10016

Copyright © text and illustrations Judith Rossell 2004
First publishing in Australia by ABC Books for the Australian Broadcasting
Corporation, GPO Box 9994, Sydney, NSW 2001.

Distributed in Canada by Sterling Publishing,
c/o Canadian Manda Group, 165 Dufferin Street
Toronto, Ontario, Canada M6K 3H6

The written instructions, photographs, designs, patterns, and projects in this volume
are intended for the personal use of the reader and may be reproduced for that pur-
pose only. Any other use, especially commercial use, is forbidden under law without
written permission of the copyright holder.

Every effort has been made to ensure that all the information in this book is accu-
rate. However, due to differing conditions, tools, and individual skills, the publisher
cannot be responsible for any injuries, losses, and other damages that may result
from the use of the information in this book.

If you have questions or comments about this book, please contact:
Lark Books
67 Broadway
Asheville, NC 28801
(828) 253-0467

Manufactured in China

All rights reserved

ISBN 13: 978-1-57990-949-9
ISBN 10: 1-57990-949-3

For information about custom editions, special sales, and premium and corporate
purchases, please contact Sterling Special Sales Department at 800-805-5489 or
specialsales@sterlingpub.com.

EXPLORERS CLUB

THE LOST TREASURE OF THE GREEN IGUANA

A JUNGLE MAZE ADVENTURE

JUDITH ROSSELL

LARK BOOKS
A Division of Sterling Publishing Co., Inc.
New York

PASADERA

*The President
Explorers' Club*

The President
Explorers' Club
99 Intrepid St.
Valeroso

Dear President,

I hope you can send one of your members to help us. Our famous scientist,
Dr. Fortuito, has disappeared. He set out a month ago on his fourteenth
expedition to seek the legendary Lost Treasure of the Green Iguana.
We are very concerned for his safety because he promised to return for
our midsummer festival and there is still no sign of him.

Attached is a recent photograph of Dr. Fortuito from the Pasadera Post.
I am also sending you a folder containing some of the doctor's notes about
the flora and fauna of this area. The jungle around Pasadera is notoriously
dangerous, but these notes will help. We are offering a huge reward for the
doctor's safe return, so please send one of your members with all speed!

Yours sincerely,

Bela Pomposo

Mrs. B. Pomposo
Mayor
Pasadera

Fourteenth Time Lucky?

"Fourteen has always been a lucky number for me," said Dr. Fortuito, before setting out today on his fourteenth expedition to find the Lost Treasure of the Green Iguana. Just released from the hospital after recovering from his thirteenth attempt, Dr. Fortuito was

EXPLORERS' CLUB

Dear Explorer,

This urgent request arrived today from the Mayor of Pasadera. A scientist, Dr. Fortuito, has vanished while searching for the Lost Treasure of the Green Iguana. With a bit of luck, you should be able to find the treasure as well as the missing scientist.

My advice is to study the doctor's folder of notes very carefully. The jungle around Pasadera is full of dangers — giant water snails, crocodiles, poisonous snakes, savage snake vines and even hippos! The notes will help you deal with anything that blocks your path.

Be prepared for a long trek — the jungle is a maze of interconnecting paths and there is no map. You will probably need to retrace your steps many times.

Best of luck for a successful expedition.

Lily Leyenda

President
Explorers' Club

Legendary Lost Treasure

The fabulous Lost Treasure of the Green Iguana is one of the greatest mysteries of our time. Originally hidden by pirates, it is believed to be in the vicinity of the ruined city of Las Cabezas. Legends tell of a ferocious Giant Green Iguana that stands guard over the treasure. The only known way to overcome this creature is to startle it away with a swarm of Red Jewel Beetles. At least 10 beetles must be collected in order to frighten away the iguana and lay claim to the treasure.

http://lostloot.com/SouthAmerica/history/legend253.asp

I found this on the Net. I hope it is useful!
Lily

Is it all clear? You need to find the lost scientist and the treasure. Use the notes on both folder flaps to help you overcome any dangers that block your way and keep your eyes open for items along the path that you will need later. When you reach the edge of a page, turn to the page number there and keep going. Do not leave the path.
Good Luck!

Start here ⟶

5→

↱3
3↳
↓5

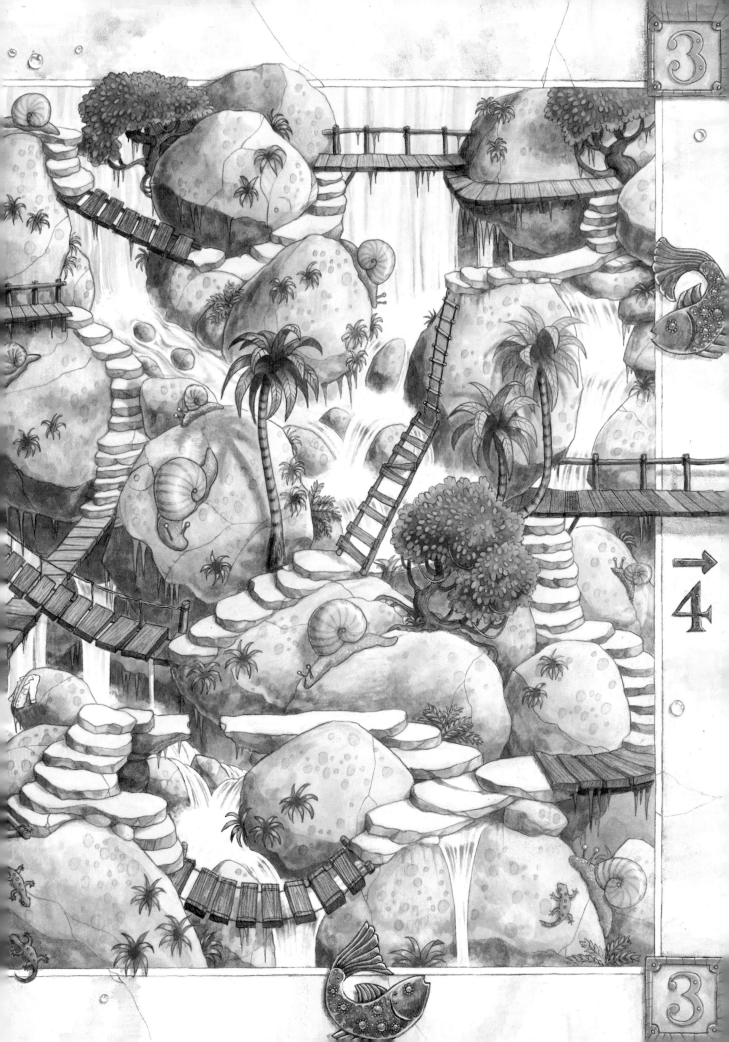

3 ←
7 ↓

→6

3 ↑
← 5
9 ↓

WHICH WAY DID YOU GO?

THE SOLUTION IS ON THE NEXT PAGE,
BUT BEFORE YOU LOOK, CAN YOU…

⇨ retrace your steps through the maze
and return to the start at Pasadera?

⇨ help find poor Dr. Fortuito's clothes?
He has lost his pith helmet, glasses, shirt,
trousers, two boots, two socks, a backpack,
and a butterfly net, which are scattered
throughout the pathways of the jungle.

⇨ find the hidden animals on each page?
Look at the animals decorating the borders
to see what is hidden in each maze.

SOLUTION

Maze 2: Collect four
Old Warty Toadstools.

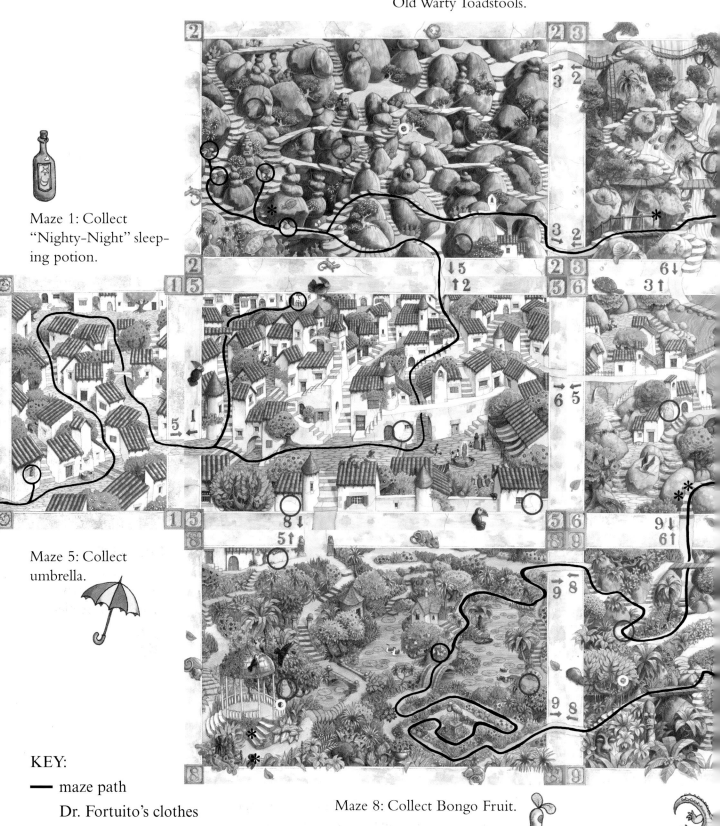

Maze 1: Collect
"Nighty-Night" sleep-
ing potion.

Maze 5: Collect
umbrella.

KEY:

— maze path

Dr. Fortuito's clothes

* Red Jewel Beetles

◯ hidden animals from maze borders (3 per maze)

Maze 8: Collect Bongo Fruit.

Maze 3: Overcome Giant Water Snails using "Nighty-Night" sleeping potion.

Maze 4: Pass Snake Vines using Old Warty Toadstools.

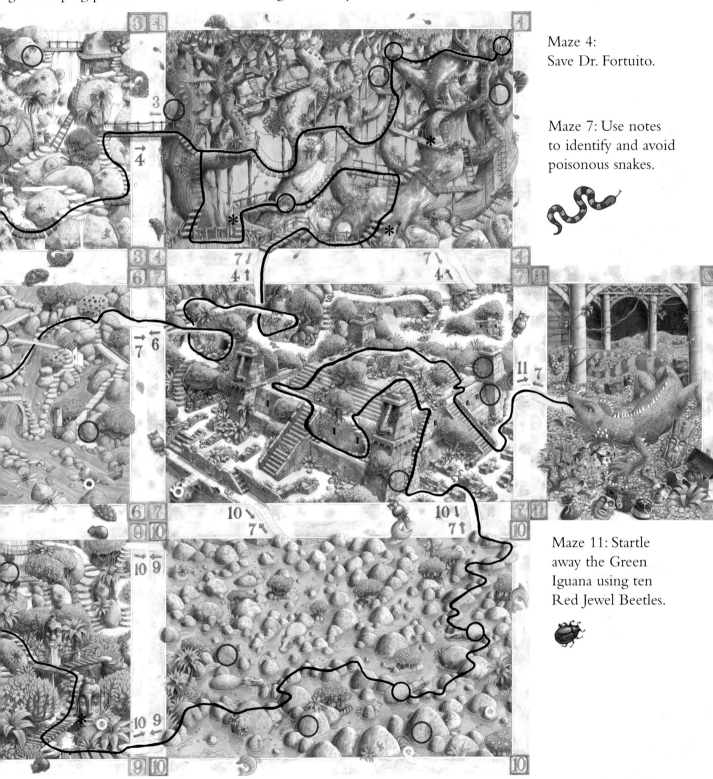

Maze 4: Save Dr. Fortuito.

Maze 7: Use notes to identify and avoid poisonous snakes.

Maze 11: Startle away the Green Iguana using ten Red Jewel Beetles.

Maze 6: Startle away crocodiles using umbrella.

Maze 10: Give Bongo Fruit to hippos and use them as stepping stones.

In the maze can you also find:

28 birds (real ones)
12 people
13 lizards (real ones)
9 monkeys
18 snails (real ones)
and
2 black cats?